RED

VERMILLION

CARMINE

THIS
BOOK BELONGS TO

MAGENTA

To Mark and Emily.

And to my editor, Ann Rider
—a ZILLION thanks.

www.houghtonmifflinbooks.com

The text of this book is set in Filosofia.
The illustrations are mixed media using Twinrocker handmade papers, collage, and found objects.

Library of Congress Cataloging-in-Publication Data

Sweet, Melissa.
Carmine : a little more red / by Melissa Sweet.
p. cm.
Summary: While a little girl who loves red—and loves to dilly-dally—
stops to paint a picture on the way to visit her grandmother,
her dog Rufus meets a wolf and unwittingly leads him directly to Granny's house.
HC ISBN-13: 978-0-618-38794-6
PA ISBN-13: 978-0-618-99717-6
[1. Red—Fiction. 2. Painting—Fiction. 3. Dogs—Fiction. 4. Wolves—Fiction.
5. Grandmothers—Fiction. 6. Conduct of life—Fiction.] I. Title.
PZ7.S9744Car 2005
[Fic]—dc22
2004009212

ISBN-13: 978-0618-38794-6

Printed in Singapore
TWP 10 9 8 7 6

Carmine and Rufus took off through the woods. They rode up
and down the hillsides until they came to the edge of a field.
There were some big tracks along the path. Rufus kept sniffing the
air. Still, Carmine thought this looked like a safe enough place—just to
stop and rest.

exquisite

It was a clear morning. The light was EXQUISITE. Carmine began making a picture for Granny.

farther

She started filling her painting with color. It may seem farfetched to think that any painting can be improved by adding a little more red, but Carmine believes it to be true. The poppies in the distance caught her eye, and she wandered FARTHER to get a better look.

green

Walking along, carrying her easel, Carmine noticed how the sunlight flickered on the tall GREEN grass, the ferns and flowers. She made sketches in her notebook. Granny would love this painting best of all.

seed pod

Papaver rhoeas

haiku

Thinking of Granny, Carmine wrote a HAIKU:

My Granny is plump.
Her soup will make you want more
The secret is bones.

indeed

Meanwhile, Rufus noticed an odd scent in the air. INDEED, he knew a wolf when he smelled one.

joke

Rufus was nervous at the thought of a wolf nearby. It is no JOKE that a wolf could eat a dog in the blink of an eye.

TYPICALLY WOLVES EAT MICE AND OTHER SMALL CREATURES.

knoll

By now Carmine was far away on a KNOLL. She could see Granny's house and even Granny's sheep way in the distance. And she could still see Rufus, but just barely.

lurking

Most wolves practice the fine art of LURKING.

mimic

A mockingbird landed above Carmine's head. Mockingbirds are famous for their ability to MIMIC sounds of all kinds; this one was snarling and growling and licking its chops. It even howled.

nincompoop

Everyone knows it isn't very nice to call a person, or even a bird, a
NINCOMPOOP, but sometimes Carmine could not help herself.

omen

The mockingbird reminded Carmine that her granny had heard a wolf howl just last night. She wondered if this bird was a sign of trouble— a bad OMEN.

pluck

Anyone else might have gotten the heebie-jeebies from a bird making sounds like that. But Carmine had a good deal of PLUCK. She rolled up her sleeves and went back to painting.

quiver

A rustling noise in the bushes made Rufus QUIVER.

reckoned

Rufus RECKONED this was a full-fledged wolf in front of him. He could tell by the large eyes, big ears, and long nose and teeth.

surreal

Rufus began to bark, and the wolf knew exactly what he was saying. SURREAL as it may seem, dogs are descendants of wolves, and it made sense that the wolf could understand his language.

It took the wolf just a little while to get to Granny's house.

trouble

As soon as Granny spotted the wolf outside, she grabbed the key to lock the door—she didn't want any TROUBLE—but it was too late.

Wwolfffff

Granny screamed at the top of her lungs. Doors slammed and pots clat-
tered. Granny saw her kitchen turned upside down. Then it went quiet.

Alphabet
Alphabet
pasta

usually

USUALLY the neighbors are home and would have heard Granny's cry for help. And usually a woodcutter is around, but on this day he was deep in the woods, felling trees for a treehouse.

voilà *

"**VOILÀ!**" Carmine had just exclaimed as she finished her painting.
It was at that moment she heard the cry—"WOLF!"

*It means "there you are, there you have it" (in French).

worry

When she heard the cry, she was filled with WORRY.
Carmine raced to Granny's as fast as she could.

x-ray

No one really has X-RAY vision except superheroes. Carmine was not a superhero. At the little white house, all she could see of Granny were her glasses flung across the floor. There were tracks and footprints, but no Granny.

Meanwhile, back at his den, the wolf held out an armful of bones. His pups began to yap their heads off.

yodel

When all hope seemed lost, Carmine and Rufus heard an odd noise—
sort of like a YODEL. The sound made Rufus berserk. Carmine yanked
on the closet door.

One day you head out down the road with no worries. The next moment, you think your granny has been eaten up by a wolf. But just as quickly— voilà!—here she is, hiding in a closet, yodeling. And everything is okay again. It's zany.

Carmine! Rufus! I'm so glad you're safe.

The wolf pushed me in the closet—goodness, it was stuffy in there.

I was too scared to come out. Then I was pretty sure I heard you two.

zillion

Granny and Carmine served up the alphabet soup. Rufus ate a bone the wolf left behind. Granny reminded Carmine that she had been told a ZILLION times not to dilly-dally in the woods. Carmine said that she would never dawdle again. She gave her granny the painting she had done, and Granny hung it on the wall with the rest of Carmine's pictures.

Carmine and Rufus zoomed home. They didn't stop once.

GRANNY'S ALPHABET SOUP

2 tablespoons olive oil

1 onion, diced

2 carrots, diced

1 green bell pepper, diced

1 celery stalk, diced

2 garlic cloves, minced

1 teaspoon oregano

1 teaspoon basil

4 cups water

1 15-ounce can tomato sauce, or 2 fresh tomatoes, chopped

½ cup alphabet pasta, uncooked

soup bones (optional)

salt and pepper

Sauté onion, carrots, pepper, celery, and garlic in olive oil for 5 minutes over medium heat. Stir in the oregano and basil.

Add water and bring to a boil. Simmer for 15–20 minutes or until vegetables are tender. (If you have bones, add them with the water.)

Add tomato sauce and pasta and simmer gently until pasta is done, about 10 more minutes.

Add salt and pepper to taste before serving, and garnish with Parmesan cheese. Voilà!

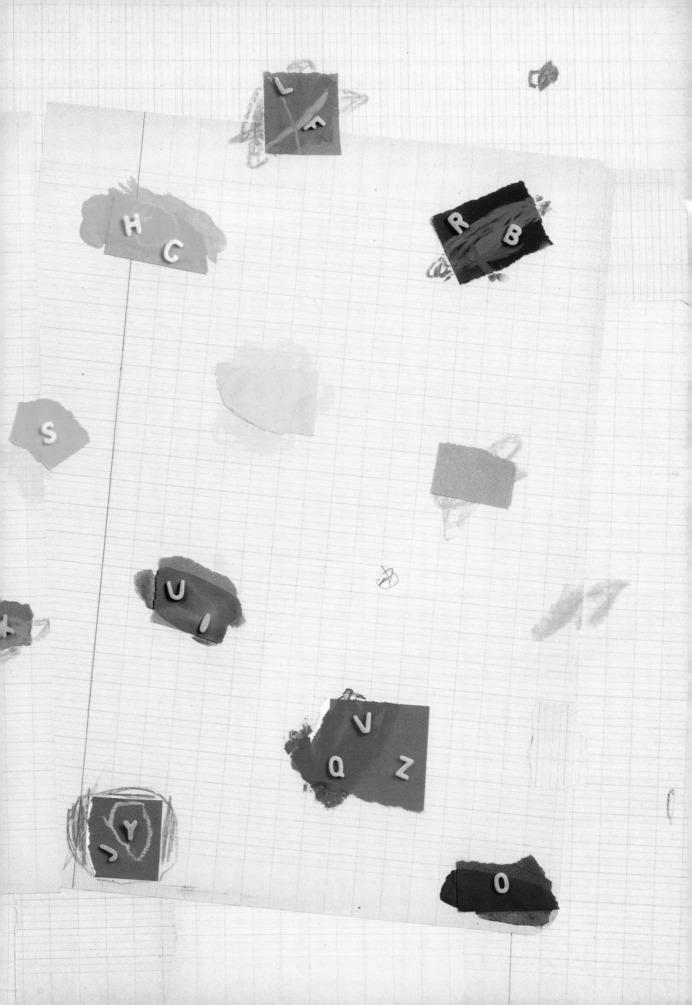